DAVID COPPERFIELD

DAVID COPPERFIELD

Abridged for Public Reading by Charles Dickens
Illustrated by Alan Marks · Afterword by Anthea Bell

A Michael Neugebauer Book

NORTH-SOUTH BOOKS · NEW YORK · LONDON

I had known Mr. Peggotty's house very well in my childhood, and I am sure I could not have been more charmed with it, if it had been Aladdin's palace, roc's egg and all. It was an old black barge or boat, high and dry on Yarmouth Sands, with an iron funnel sticking out of it for a chimney. There was a delightful door cut in the side, and it was roofed in, and there were little windows in it. It was beautifully clean and as tidy as possible. There were some lockers and boxes, and there was a table, and there was a Dutch clock, and there was a chest of drawers, and there was a tea-tray with a painting on it, and the tray was kept from tumbling down, by a Bible; and the tray, if it had tumbled down, would have smashed a quantity of cups and saucers and a teapot that were grouped around the book. On the walls were coloured pictures of Abraham in red going to sacrifice Isaac in blue; and of Daniel in yellow being cast into a den of green lions. Mr. Peggotty, as honest a seafaring man as ever breathed, dealt in lobsters, crabs and crawfish.

As in my childhood, so in these days when I was a young man, Mr. Peggotty's household consisted of his orphan nephew Ham Peggotty, a young shipwright; his adopted niece Little Emily, once my small sweetheart, now a beautiful young woman; and Mrs. Gummidge. All three had been maintained at Mr. Peggotty's sole charge for years and years; and Mrs. Gummidge was the widow of his partner in a boat, who had died poor. She was very grateful, but she certainly would have been more agreeable if she had not constantly complained, as she sat in the most comfortable corner by the fireside, that she was a "lone lorn creetur and everythink went contrairy with her."

Towards this old boat, I walked one memorable night, with my former schoolfellow and present dear friend, Steerforth; Steerforth, half a dozen years older than I; brilliant, handsome, easy, winning; whom I admired with my whole heart; for whom I entertained the most romantic feelings of fidelity and friendship. He had come down with me from London, and had entered with the greatest ardour into my scheme of visiting the old simple place and the old simple people.

There was no moon; and as he and I walked on the dark wintry sands towards the old boat, the wind sighed mournfully.

"This is a wild place, Steerforth, is it not?"

"Dismal enough in the dark, and the sea has a cry in it, as if it were hungry for us. Is that the boat, where I see a light yonder?"

"That's the boat."

We said no more as we approached the light, but made softly for the door. I laid my hand upon the latch; and whispering Steerforth to keep close to me, went in, and I was in the midst of the astonished family, whom I had not seen from my childhood, face to face with Mr. Peggotty, and holding out my hand to him, when Ham shouted:

"Mas'r Davy! It's Mas'r Davy!"

In a moment we were all shaking hands with one another, and asking one another how we did, and telling one another how glad we were to meet, and all talking at once. Mr. Peggotty was so overjoyed to see me, and to see my friend, that he did not know what to say or do, but kept over and over again shaking hands with me, and then with Steerforth, and then with me, and then ruffling his shaggy hair all over his head, and then laughing with such glee and triumph, that it was a treat to see him.

"Why, that you two gentl'men – gentl'men growed – should come to this here roof to-night, of all nights in my life, is such a merry-go-rounder as never happened afore, I do rightly believe! Em'ly, my darling, come here! Come here, my little witch! Theer's Mas'r Davy's friend, my dear! Theer's the gentl'man as you've heerd on, Em'ly. He comes to see you, along with Mas'r Davy, on the brightest night of your uncle's life as ever was or will be, horroar for it!" Then he let her go; and as she ran into her little chamber, looked round upon us, quite hot and out of breath with his uncommon satisfaction.

"If you two gentl'men – gentl'men growed now, and such gentl'men – don't ex-cuse me for being in a state of mind, when you understand matters, I'll arks your pardon. Em'ly, my dear! – She knows I'm agoing to tell, and has made off. This here little Em'ly, sir," to Steerforth,

"– her as you see a blushing here just now – this here little Em'ly of ours, has been, in our house, sir, what I suppose (I'm a ignorant man, but that's my belief) no one but a little bright-eyed creetur *can* be in a house. She ain't my child; I never had one; but I couldn't love her more, if she was fifty times my child. You understand! I couldn't do it!"

"I quite understand."

"I know you do, sir, and thank'ee. Well, Sir, there was a certain person as had know'd our Em'ly, from the time when her father was drownded; as had seen her constant when a babby, when a young gal, when a woman. Not much of a person to look at, he warn't – something o' my own build – rough – a good deal o' the sou'wester in him – wery salt – but, on the whole, a honest sort of a chap too, with his art in the right place."

I had never seen Ham grin to anything like the extent to which he sat grinning at us now.

"What does this here blessed tarpaulin go and do, but he loses that there art of his to our little Em'ly. He follers her about, he makes hisself a sort o' servant to her, he loses in a great measure his relish for his wittles, and in the long run he makes it clear to me wot's amiss. Well! I counsels him to speak to Em'ly. He's big enough, but he's bashfuller than a little un, and he says to me he doen't like. So I speak. 'What! Him!' says Em'ly. 'Him that I've know'd so intimate so many year, and like so much! Oh, Uncle! I never can have him. He's such a good fellow!' I gives her a kiss, and I says no more to her than 'My dear, you're right to speak out, you're to choose for yourself, you're as free as a little bird.' Then I aways to him, and I says, 'I wish it could have been so, but it can't. But you can both be as you was, and wot I say to you is, Be as you was with her, like a man.' He says to me, a shaking of my hand, 'I will!' he says. And he was – honourable, trew, and manful – going on for two year.

"All of a sudden, one evening – as it might be to-night – comes little Em'ly from her work, and him with her! There ain't so much in that, you'll say. No, sure, because he takes care on her, like a brother, arter dark, and indeed afore dark, and at all times. But this heer tarpaulin chap, he takes hold of her hand, and he cries out to me, joyful, 'Lookee here! This is to be my little wife!' And she says, half bold and half shy, and half a laughing and half a crying, 'Yes, uncle! If you please.' – If I please! Lord, as if I should do anythink else! – 'If you please,' she says, 'I am steadier now, and I have thought better of it, and I'll be as good a little wife as I can to him, for he's a dear good fellow!'

Then Missis Gummidge, she claps her hands like a play, and you come in. There! The murder's out! You come in! It took place this here present hour; and here's the man as'll marry her, the minute she's out of her time at the needlework."

Ham staggered, as well he might, under the blow Mr. Peggotty dealt him, as a mark of confidence and friendship; but feeling called upon to say something to us, he stammered:

"She warn't no higher than you was, Mas'r Davy – when you first come heer – when I thought what she'd grow up to be. I see her grow up – gentl'men – like a flower. I'd lay down my life for her – Mas'r Davy – Oh! most content and cheerful! There ain't a gentl'man in all the land –

13

nor yet a sailing upon all the sea – that can love his lady more than I love her, though there's many a common man – as could say better – what he meant."

I thought it affecting to see such a sturdy fellow trembling in the strength of what he felt for the pretty little creature who had won his heart. I thought the simple confidence reposed in us by Mr. Peggotty and by himself, was touching. I was affected by the story altogether. I was filled with pleasure; but at first, with an indescribably sensitive pleasure, that a very little would have changed to pain.

Therefore, if it had depended upon me to touch the prevailing chord among them with any skill, I should have made a poor hand of it. But it depended upon Steerforth; and he did it with such address, that in a few minutes we were all as easy as possible.

"Mr. Peggotty," he said, "you are a thoroughly good fellow, and deserve to be as happy as you are to-night. My hand upon it! Ham, I give you joy, my boy. My hand upon that, too! Davy, stir the fire, and make it a brisk one! And Mr. Peggotty, unless you can induce your gentle niece to come back, I shall go. Any gap at your fireside on such a night – such a gap least of all – I wouldn't make, for the wealth of the Indies!"

So, Mr. Peggotty went to fetch little Em'ly. At first little Em'ly didn't like to come, and then Ham went. Presently they brought her to the fireside, very much confused, and very shy, – but she soon became more assured when she found how Steerforth spoke to her; how skilfully he avoided anything that would embarrass her; how he talked to Mr. Peggotty of boats, and ships, and tides, and fish; how delighted he was with that boat and all belonging to it; how lightly and easily he carried on, until he brought us, by degrees, into a charmed circle.

But he set up no monopoly of the conversation. He was silent and attentive when little Emily talked across the fire to me of our old childish wanderings upon the beach, to pick up shells and pebbles; he was very silent and attentive, when I asked her if she recollected how I used to love her, and how we used to walk about that dim old flat, hours and hours, and how the days sported by us as if Time himself had not grown up then, but were a child like ourselves, and always at play. She sat all the evening, in her old little corner by the fire – Ham beside her.

I could not satisfy myself whether it was in her little tormenting way, or in a maidenly reserve before us, that she kept quite close to the wall, and away from Ham; but I observed that she did so, all the evening.

As I remember, it was almost midnight when we took our leave. We had had some biscuit and dried fish for supper, and Steerforth had produced from his pocket a flask of Hollands. We parted merrily; and as they all stood crowded round the door to light us on our road,

I saw the sweet blue eyes of little Em'ly peeping after us, from behind Ham, and heard her soft voice calling to us to be careful how we went.

"A most engaging little Beauty!" said Steerforth, taking my arm. "Well! It's a quaint place, and they are quaint company; and it's quite a new sensation to mix with them."

"How fortunate we are, too, Steerforth, to have arrived to witness their happiness in that intended marriage! I never saw people so happy. How delightful to see it!"

"Yes – that's rather a chuckle-headed fellow for the girl. Isn't he?"

I felt a shock in this cold reply. But turning quickly upon him, and seeing a laugh in his eyes, I answered:

"Ah, Steerforth! It's well for you to joke about the poor! But when I see how perfectly you understand them, and how you can enter into happiness like this plain fisherman's, I know there is not a joy, or sorrow, or any emotion, of such people, that can be indifferent to you. And I admire and love you for it, Steerforth, twenty times the more!"

To my surprise, he suddenly said, with nothing, that I could see, to lead to it:

"Daisy, I wish to God I had had a judicious father these last twenty years! You know my mother has always doted on me and spoilt me. I wish with all my soul I had been better guided! I wish with all my soul, I could guide myself better!"

There was a passionate dejection in his manner that quite amazed me. He was more unlike himself than I could have supposed possible.

"It would be better to be this poor Peggotty, or his lout of a nephew, than be myself, twenty times richer and twenty times wiser, and be the torment to myself that I have been in that Devil's bark of a boat within the last half-hour."

I was so confounded by the change in him that at first I could only regard him in silence as he walked at my side. At length I asked him to tell me what had happened to cross him so unusually.

"Tut, it's nothing – nothing, Davy! I must have had a nightmare, I think. What old women call the horrors, have been creeping over me from head to foot. I have been afraid of myself."

"You are afraid of nothing else, I think."

"Perhaps not, and yet may have enough to be afraid of, too. Well! so it goes by! Daisy – for though that's not the name your godfathers and godmothers gave you, you're such a fresh fellow that it's the name I best like to call you by – and I wish, I wish, I wish, you could give it to me!"

"Why, so I can, if I choose."

"Daisy, if anything should ever happen to separate us, you must think of me at my best, old boy. Come! let us make that bargain. Think of me at my best, if circumstances should ever part us!"

"You have no best to me, Steerforth, and no worst. You are always equally loved and cherished in my heart."

I was up, to go away alone, next morning with the dawn, and, having dressed as quietly as I could, looked into his room. He was fast asleep; lying, easily, with his head upon his arm, as I had often seen him lie at school.

The time came in its season, and that was very soon, when I almost wondered that nothing troubled his repose, as I looked at him then. But he slept — let me think of him so again — as I had often seen him sleep at school; and thus, in this silent hour I left him.

– Never more, O God forgive you, Steerforth! to touch that passive hand in love and friendship. Never, never, more!

CHAPTER II

Some months elapsed, before I again found myself down in that part of the country, and approaching the old boat by night.

It was a dark evening, and rain was beginning to fall, when I came within sight of Mr. Peggotty's house, and of the light within it shining through the window. A little floundering across the sand, which was heavy, brought me to the door, and I went in. I was bidden to a little supper; Emily was to be married to Ham that day fortnight, and this was the last time I was to see her in her maiden life.

It looked very comfortable, indeed. Mr. Peggotty had smoked his evening pipe, and there were preparations for supper by-and-by. The fire was bright, the ashes were thrown up, the locker was ready for little Emily in her old place. Mrs. Gummidge appeared to be fretting a little, in her own corner: and consequently looked quite natural.

"You're first of the lot, Mas'r Davy! Sit ye down, sir. It ain't o' no use saying welcome to you, but you're welcome, kind and hearty."

Here Mrs. Gummidge groaned.

"Cheer up, cheer up, Mrs. Gummidge!" said Mr. Peggotty.

"No, no, Dan'l. It ain't o' no use telling me to cheer up, when everythink goes contrairy with me. Nothink's nat'ral to me but to be lone and lorn."

After looking at Mrs. Gummidge for some moments, with great sympathy, Mr. Peggotty glanced at the Dutch clock, rose, snuffed the candle, and put it in the window.

"Theer! Theer we are, Missis Gummidge!" Mrs. Gummidge slightly groaned again. "Theer we are, Mrs. Gummidge, lighted up, accordin' to custom! You're a wonderin' what that's fur, sir! Well, it's fur our little Em'ly. You see, the path ain't over light or cheerful arter dark; and when I'm here at the hour as she's a comin' home from her needlework down-town, I puts the light in the winder. That, you see, meets two objects. She says to herself, says Em'ly, 'Theer's home!' she says. And likeways, says Em'ly, 'My uncle's theer!' Fur if I ain't theer, I never have no light showed. You may say this is like a Babby, sir. Well, I doen't know but what I am a babby in regard o' Em'ly. Not to look at, but to – to consider on, you know. *I* doen't care, bless you! Now I tell you. When I go a looking and looking about that theer pritty house of our Em'ly's, all got ready for her to be married, if I doen't feel as if the littlest things was her, a'most. I takes 'em up, and I puts 'em down, and I touches of 'em as delicate as if they was our Em'ly. So 't is with her little bonnets and that. I couldn't see one on 'em rough used a purpose – not fur the whole wureld.

"It's my opinion, you see, as this is along of my havin' played with Em'ly so much when she was a child, and havin' made believe as we was Turks, and French, and sharks, and every wariety of forinners – bless you, yes; and lions and whales, and I don't know what all! – when she warn't no higher than my knee. I've got into the way on it, you know. Why, this here candle, now! *I* know wery well that arter she's married and gone, I shall put that candle theer, just the same as now, and sit afore the fire, pretending I'm expecting of her, like as I'm a doing now. Why, at the present minute, when I see the candle sparkle up, I says to myself, 'She's a looking at it! Em'ly's a coming!' Right too, fur here she is!"

No; it was only Ham. The night should have turned more wet since I came in, for he had a large sou'wester hat on, slouched over his face.

"Where's Em'ly?"

Ham made a movement, as if she were outside. Mr. Peggotty took the light from the window, trimmed it, put it on the table, and was stirring the fire, when Ham, who had not moved, said:

"Mas'r Davy, will you come out a minute, and see what Em'ly and me has got to show you?"

As I passed him, I saw, to my astonishment and fright, that he was deadly pale. He closed the door upon us. Only upon us two.

"Ham! What's the matter?"

"My love, Mas'r Davy – the pride and hope of my art – her that I'd have died for, and would die for now – she's gone!"

"Gone!"

"Em'ly's run away! You're a scholar, and know what's right and best. What am I to say, in-doors? How am I ever to break it to him, Mas'r Davy?"

21

I saw the door move, and tried to hold the latch, to gain a moment's time. It was too late. Mr. Peggotty thrust forth his face; and never could I forget the change that came upon it when he saw us; if I were to live five hundred years.

I remember a great wail and cry, and the women hanging about him, and we all standing in the room; I with an open letter in my hand, which Ham had given me; Mr. Peggotty, with his vest torn open, his hair wild, his face and lips white, and blood trickling down his bosom (it had sprung from his mouth, I think).

"Read it, sir; slow, please. I doen't know as I can understand."

In the midst of the silence of death, I read thus, from the blotted letter Ham had given me. In Em'ly's hand – addressed to himself:

"'When you, who love me so much better than I ever have deserved, even when my mind was innocent, see this, I shall be far away. When I leave my dear home – my dear home – oh, my dear home! – in the morning,'" – the letter bore date on the previous night: "'– it will be never to come back, unless he brings me back a lady. This will be found at night, many hours after, instead of me. For mercy's sake, tell uncle that I never loved him half so dear as now. Oh, don't remember you and I were ever to be married – but try to think as if I died when I was little, and was buried somewhere. Pray Heaven that I am going away from, have compassion on my uncle! Be his comfort. Love some good girl, that will be what I was once to uncle, and that will be true to you, and worthy of you, and know no shame but me. God bless all! If he don't bring me back a lady, and I don't pray for my own self, I'll pray for all. My parting love to uncle. My last tears, and my last thanks, for uncle!'"

That was all. He stood, long after I had ceased to read, still looking at me. Slowly, at last, he moved his eyes from my face, and cast them round the room.

"Who's the man? I want to know his name."

Ham glanced at me, and suddenly I felt a shock.

"Mas'r Davy! Go out a bit, and let me tell him what I must. You doen't ought to hear it, sir."

I sank down in a chair, and tried to utter some reply; but my tongue was fettered, and my sight was weak. For I felt that the man was my friend – the friend I had unhappily introduced there – Steerforth, my old schoolfellow and my friend.

"I want to know his name!"

"Mas'r Davy's friend. He's the man. Mas'r Davy, it ain't no fault of yourn – and I am far from laying of it to you – but it is your friend Steerforth, and he's a damned villain!"

Mr. Peggotty moved no more, until he seemed to wake all at once, and pulled down his rough coat from its peg in a corner.

23

"Bear a hand with this! I'm struck of a heap, and can't do it. Bear a hand, and help me. Well!
Now give me that theer hat!"

Ham asked him whither he was going?

"I'm a going to seek my niece. I'm a going to seek my Em'ly. I'm a going, first, to stave in that
theer boat as he gave me, and sink it where I would have drownded *him,* as I'm a livin' soul,
if I had had one thought of what was in him! As he sat afore me, in that boat, face to face,
strike me down dead, but I'd have drownded him, and thought it right! – I'm a going fur to
seek my niece."

"Where?"

"Anywhere! I'm a going to seek my niece through the wureld. I'm a going to find my poor niece
in her shame, and bring her back wi' my comfort and forgiveness. No one stop me! I tell you
I'm a going to seek my niece! I'm a going to seek her fur and wide!"

Mrs. Gummidge came between them, in a fit of crying. "No, no, Dan'l, not as you are now.
Seek her in a little while, my lone lorn Dan'l, and that'll be but right; but not as you are now.
Sit ye down, and give me your forgiveness for having ever been a worrit to you, Dan'l – what
have *my* contrairies ever been to this! – and let us speak a word about them times when she
was first a orphan, and when Ham was too, and when I was a poor widder woman, and you
took me in. It'll soften your poor heart, Dan'l, and you'll bear your sorrow better; for you know
the promise, Dan'l, 'As you have done it unto one of the least of these, you have done it unto
me;' and that can never fail under this roof, that's been our shelter for so many, many year!"

He was quite passive now; and when I heard him crying, the impulse that had been upon me
to go down upon my knees, and curse Steerforth, yielded to a better feeling. My overcharged
heart found the same relief as his, and I cried too.

CHAPTER III

At this period of my life I lived in my top set of chambers in Buckingham Street, Strand, London, and was over head and ears in love with Dora. I lived principally on Dora and coffee. My appetite languished and I was glad of it, for I felt as though it would have been an act of perfidy towards Dora to have a natural relish for my dinner. I bought four sumptuous waist-coats – not for myself; *I* had no pride in them – for Dora. I took to wearing straw-coloured kid gloves in the streets. I laid the foundations of all the corns I have ever had. If the boots I wore at that period could only be produced and compared with the natural size of my feet, they would show in a most affecting manner what the state of my heart was.

Mrs. Crupp, the housekeeper of my chambers, must have been a woman of penetration; for, when this attachment was but a few weeks old, she found it out. She came up to me one evening when I was very low, to ask (she being afflicted with spasms) if I could oblige her with a little tincture of cardamums, mixed with rhubarb and flavoured with seven drops of the essence of cloves – or, if I had not such a thing by me – with a little brandy. As I had never even heard of the first remedy, and always had the second in the closet, I gave Mrs. Crupp a glass of the second; which (that I might have no suspicion of its being devoted to any improper use) she began to take immediately.

"Cheer up, sir," said Mrs. Crupp. "Excuse me. I know what it is, sir. There's a lady in the case."

"Mrs. Crupp?"

"Oh, bless you! Keep a good heart, sir! Never say die, sir! If she don't smile upon you, there's a many as will. You're a young gentleman to *be* smiled on, Mr. Copperfull, and you must learn your walue, sir."

Mrs. Crupp always called me Mr. Copperfull: firstly, no doubt, because it was not my name; and secondly, I am inclined to think, in some indistinct association with a washing-day.

"What makes you suppose there is any young lady in the case, Mrs. Crupp?"

"Mr. Copperfull, I'm a mother myself. Your boots and your waist is equally too small, and you don't eat enough, sir, nor yet drink. Sir, I have laundressed other young gentlemen besides you. It was but the gentleman which died here before yourself, that fell in love – with a barmaid – and had his waistcoats took in directly, though much swelled by drinking."

"Mrs. Crupp, I must beg you not to connect the young lady in my case with a barmaid, or anything of that sort, if you please."

"Mr. Copperfull, I'm a mother myself, and not likely. I ask your pardon, sir, if I intrude. I should never wish to intrude where I were not welcome. But you are a young gentleman, Mr. Copperfull, and my adwice to you is, to cheer up, sir, to keep a good heart, and to know your own walue. If you was to take to something, sir; if you was to take to skittles, now, which is healthy, you might find it divert your mind, and do you good."

I turned it off and changed the subject by informing Mrs. Crupp that I wished to entertain at dinner next day, my esteemed friends Traddles, and Mr. and Mrs. Micawber. And I took the liberty of suggesting a pair of soles, a small leg of mutton, and a pigeon pie. Mrs. Crupp broke out into rebellion on my first bashful hint in reference to her cooking the fish and joint. But, in the end, a compromise was effected; and Mrs. Crupp consented to achieve this feat, on condition that I dined from home for a fortnight afterwards.

Having laid in the materials for a bowl of punch, to be compounded by Mr. Micawber; having provided a bottle of lavender-water, two wax candles, a paper of mixed pins, and a pin-cushion, to assist Mrs. Micawber in her toilette, at my dressing-table; having also caused the fire in my bed-room to be lighted for Mrs. Micawber's convenience; and having laid the cloth with my own hands; I awaited the result with composure.

At the appointed time, my three visitors arrived together. Mr. Micawber with more shirt-collar than usual, and a new ribbon to his eye-glass; Mrs. Micawber with her cap in a parcel; Traddles carrying the parcel, and supporting Mrs. Micawber on his arm. They were all delighted with my residence. When I conducted Mrs. Micawber to my dressing-table, and she saw the scale on which it was prepared for her, she was in such raptures, that she called Mr. Micawber to come in and look.

"My dear Copperfield," said Mr. Micawber, "this is luxurious. This is a way of life which reminds me of the period when I was myself in a state of celibacy. I am at present established on what may be designated as a small and unassuming scale; but, you are aware that I have, in the course of my career, surmounted difficulties, and conquered obstacles. You are no stranger to the fact, that there have been periods of my life, when it has been requisite that

I should pause, until certain expected events should turn up – when it has been necessary that I should fall back, before making what I trust I shall not be accused of presumption in terming – a spring. The present is one of those momentous stages in the life of man. You find me, fallen back, *for* a spring; and I have every reason to believe that a vigorous leap will shortly be the result."

I informed Mr. Micawber that I relied upon him for a bowl of punch, and led him to the lemons. I never saw a man so thoroughly enjoy himself, as he stirred, and mixed, and tasted, and looked as if he were making, not mere punch, but a fortune for his family down to the latest posterity. As to Mrs. Micawber, I don't know whether it was the effect of the cap, or the lavender-water, or the pins, or the fire, or the wax-candles, but she came out of my room, comparatively speaking, lovely.

I suppose – I never ventured to inquire, but I suppose – that Mrs. Crupp, after frying the soles, was taken ill. Because we broke down at that point. The leg of mutton came up, very red inside, and very pale outside: besides having a foreign substance of a gritty nature sprinkled over it, as if it had had a fall into ashes. But we were not in a condition to judge of this fact from the appearance of the gravy, forasmuch as it had been all dropped on the stairs. The pigeon-pie was not bad, but it was a delusive pie: the crust being like a disappointing phrenological head: full of lumps and bumps, with nothing particular underneath. In short, the banquet was such a failure that I should have been quite unhappy – about the failure, I mean, for I was always unhappy about Dora – if I had not been relieved by the great good-humour of my company.

"My dear friend Copperfield," said Mr. Micawber, "accidents will occur in the best-regulated families; and especially in families not regulated by that pervading influence which sanctifies while it enhances the – a – I would say, in short, by the influence of Woman in the lofty character of Wife. If you will allow me to take the liberty of remarking that there are few comestibles better, in their way, than a Devil, and that I believe, with a little division of labour, we could accomplish a good one if the young person in attendance could produce a gridiron, I would put it to you, that this little misfortune may be easily repaired."

There was a gridiron in the pantry, on which my morning rasher of bacon was cooked. We had it out, in a twinkling; Traddles cut the mutton into slices; Mr. Micawber covered them with pepper, mustard, salt, and cayenne; I put them on the gridiron, turned them with a fork, and took them off, under Mr. Micawber's direction; and Mrs. Micawber heated some mushroom ketchup in a little saucepan. Under these circumstances, my appetite came back miraculously. I am ashamed to confess it, but I really believe I forgot Dora for a little while.

"Punch, my dear Copperfield," said Mr. Micawber, tasting it as soon as dinner was done, "like time and tide, waits for no man. Ah! it is at the present moment in high flavour. My love, will you give me your opinion?"

Mrs. Micawber pronounced it excellent.

"As we are quite confidential here, Mr. Copperfield," said Mrs. Micawber sipping her punch, "(Mr. Traddles being a part of our domesticity), I should much like to have your opinion on Mr. Micawber's prospects. I have consulted branches of my family on the course most expedient for Mr. Micawber to take, and it was, that he should immediately turn his attention to coals."

"To what, ma'am?"

"To coals. To the coal trade. Mr. Micawber was induced to think on inquiry, that there might be an opening for a man of his talent in the Medway Coal Trade. Then, as Mr. Micawber very properly said, the first step to be taken clearly was, to go and see the Medway. Which we went and saw. I say 'we,' Mr. Copperfield; for I never will desert Mr. Micawber. I am a wife and mother, and I never will desert Mr. Micawber."

Traddles and I murmured our admiration.

"That," said Mrs. Micawber, "that, at least, is my view, my dear Mr. Copperfield and Mr. Traddles, of the obligation which I took upon myself when I repeated the irrevocable words 'I Emma, take thee, Wilkins.' I read the service over with a flat-candle, on the previous night, and the conclusion I derived from it was that I never could or would desert Mr. Micawber."

"My dear," said Mr. Micawber, a little impatiently, "I am not conscious that you are expected to do anything of the sort."

"We went," repeated Mrs. Micawber, "and saw the Medway. My opinion of the coal trade on that river, was, that it might require talent, but that it certainly requires capital. Talent, Mr. Micawber has; capital, Mr. Micawber has not. We saw, I think, the greater part of the Medway; and that was my individual conclusion. My family were then of opinion that Mr. Micawber should turn his attention to corn – on commission. But corn, as I have repeatedly said to Mr. Micawber, may be gentlemanly, but it is not remunerative. Commission to the extent of two and ninepence in a fortnight cannot, however limited our ideas, be considered remunerative."

We were all agreed upon that.

"Then," said Mrs. Micawber, who prided herself on taking a clear view of things, and keeping Mr. Micawber straight by her woman's wisdom, when he might otherwise go a little crooked, "then I naturally look round the world, and say, 'What is there in which a person of Mr. Micawber's talent is likely to succeed?' I may have a conviction that Mr. Micawber's manners peculiarly qualify him for the Banking business. I may argue within myself, that if I had a deposit at a banking-house, the manners of Mr. Micawber, as representing that banking-house, would inspire confidence, and extend the connexion. But if the various banking-houses refuse to avail themselves of Mr. Micawber's abilities, or receive the offer of them with contumely, what is the use of dwelling upon *that* idea? None. As to originating a banking-business, I may know that there are members of my family who, if they chose to place their money in Mr. Micawber's hands, might found an establishment of that description. But if they do *not* choose to place their money in Mr. Micawber's hands – which they don't – what is the use of that? Again I contend that we are no farther advanced than we were before."

I shook my head, and said, "Not a bit." Traddles also shook his head, and said, "Not a bit."

"What do I deduce from this?" Mrs. Micawber went on to say, still with the same air of putting a case lucidly.

"What is the conclusion, my dear Mr. Copperfield, to which I am irresistibly brought? Am I wrong in saying, it is clear that we must live?"

I answered, "Not at all!" and Traddles answered, "Not at all!" and I found myself afterwards sagely adding, alone, that a person must either live or die.

"Just so," returned Mrs. Micawber. "It is precisely that. And here is Mr. Micawber without any suitable position or employment. Where does that responsibility rest? Clearly on society. Then I would make a fact so disgraceful known, and boldly challenge society to set it right. It appears to me, my dear Mr. Copperfield, that what Mr. Micawber has to do is to throw down the gauntlet to society, and say, in effect, 'Show me who will take that up. Let the party immediately step forward.' It appears to me, that what Mr. Micawber has to do, is to advertise in all the papers; to describe himself plainly as so and so, with such and such qualifications, and to put it thus: '*Now* employ me, on remunerative terms, and address, post paid, to *W. M.,* Post Office, Camden Town.' For this purpose, I think Mr. Micawber ought to raise a certain sum of money – on a bill. If no member of my family is possessed of sufficient natural feeling to negotiate that bill, then, my opinion is, that Mr. Micawber should go into the City, should take that bill into the Money Market, and should dispose of it for what he can get."

I felt, but I am sure I don't know why, that this was highly self-denying and devoted in Mrs. Micawber, and I uttered a murmur to that effect. Traddles, who took his tone from me, did likewise, and really I felt that she was a noble woman – the sort of woman who might have been a Roman matron, and done all manner of troublesome heroic public actions.

In the fervour of this impression, I congratulated Mr. Micawber on the treasure he possessed. So did Traddles. Mr. Micawber extended his hand to each of us in succession, and then covered his face with his pocket-handkerchief – which I think had more snuff upon it than he was aware of. He then returned to the punch in the highest state of exhilaration.

Mrs. Micawber made tea for us in a most agreeable manner; and after tea we discussed a variety of topics before the fire; and she was good enough to sing us (in a small, thin, flat voice, which I remembered to have considered, when I first knew her, the very table-beer of acoustics) the favourite ballads of "The Dashing White Sergeant," and "Little Tafflin." For both of these songs Mrs. Micawber had been famous when she lived at home with her papa and mamma. Mr. Micawber told us, that when he heard her sing the first one, on the first occasion of his seeing her beneath the parental roof, she had attracted his attention in an extraordinary degree; but that when it came to Little Tafflin, he had resolved to win that woman, or perish in the attempt.

It was between ten and eleven o'clock when Mrs. Micawber rose to replace her cap in the parcel, and to put on her bonnet. Mr. Micawber took the opportunity to slip a letter into my hand, with a whispered request that I would read it at my leisure. I also took the opportunity of my holding a candle over the bannisters to light them down, when Mr. Micawber was going first, leading Mrs. Micawber, to detain Traddles for a moment on the top of the stairs.

"Traddles, Mr. Micawber don't mean any harm; but, if I were you, I wouldn't lend him anything."

"My dear Copperfield, I haven't got anything to lend."

"You have got a name, you know."

"Oh! you call *that* something to lend?"

"Certainly."

"Oh! Yes, to be sure! I am very much obliged to you, Copperfield, but – I am afraid I have lent him that already."

"For the bill that is to go into the Money Market?"

"No. Not for that one. This is the first I have heard of that one. I have been thinking that he will most likely propose that one, on the way home. Mine's another."

"I hope there will be nothing wrong about it."

"I hope not. I should think not, though, because he told me, only the other day, that it was provided for. That was Mr. Micawber's expression, 'Provided for.'"

Mr. Micawber looking up at this juncture, I had only time to repeat my caution. Traddles thanked me, and descended. But I was much afraid, when I observed the good-natured manner in which he went down with Mrs. Micawber's cap in his hand, that he would be carried into the Money Market, neck and heels.

I returned to my fireside, and read Mr. Micawber's letter, which was dated an hour and a half before dinner. I am not sure whether I have mentioned that, when Mr. Micawber was at any particularly desperate crisis, he used a sort of legal phraseology: which he seemed to think equivalent to winding up his affairs.

This was the letter.

"Sir – for I dare not say my dear Copperfield,

"It is expedient that I should inform you that the undersigned is Crushed. Some flickering efforts to spare you the premature knowledge of his calamitous position, you may observe in him this day; but hope has sunk beneath the horizon, and the undersigned is Crushed.

"The present communication is penned within the personal range (I cannot call it the society) of an individual, in a state closely bordering on intoxication, employed by a broker. That individual is in legal possession of the premises, under a distress for rent. His inventory

includes, not only the chattels and effects of every description belonging to the undersigned, as yearly tenant of this habitation, but also those appertaining to Mr. Thomas Traddles, lodger, a member of the Honourable Society of the Inner Temple.

"If any drop of gloom were wanting in the overflowing cup, which is now 'commended' (in the language of an immortal Writer) to the lips of the undersigned, it would be found in the fact, that a friendly acceptance granted to the undersigned, by the before-mentioned Mr. Thomas Traddles, for the sum of £23 4s. 9½ *d.,* is over due, and is NOT provided for. Also, in the fact, that the living responsibilities clinging to the undersigned will, in the course of nature, be increased by the sum of one more helpless victim; whose miserable appearance may be looked for – in round numbers – at the expiration of a period not exceeding six lunar months from the present date.

"After premising thus much, it would be a work of supererogation to add, that dust and ashes are for ever scattered

"On

   "The

      "Head

         "Of

           "WILKINS MICAWBER."

CHAPTER IV

Seldom did I wake at night, seldom did I look up at the moon or stars or watch the falling rain, or hear the wind, but I thought of the solitary figure of the good fisherman toiling on – poor Pilgrim! – and recalled his words, "I'm a going to seek my niece. I'm a going to seek her fur and wide."

Months passed, and he had been absent – no one knew where – the whole time.

It had been a bitter day in London, and a cutting north-east wind had blown. The wind had gone down with the light, and snow had come on. My shortest way home, – and I naturally took the shortest way on such a night – was through Saint Martin's Lane. On the steps of the church, there was the figure of a man. And I stood face to face with Mr. Peggotty!

"Mas'r Davy! It do my art good to see you, sir. Well met, well met!"

"Well met, my dear old friend!"

"I had thowts o' coming to make inquiration for you, sir, to-night, but it was too late. I should have come early in the morning, sir, afore going away agen."

"Again?"

"Yes, sir, I'm away to-morrow."

In those days there was a side entrance to the stable-yard of the Golden Cross Inn. Two or three public-rooms opened out of the yard: and looking into one of them, and finding it empty, and a good fire burning, I took him in there.

"I'll tell you, Mas'r Davy, wheer-all I've been, and what-all we've heerd. I've been fur, and we've heerd little; but I'll tell you!"

As he sat thinking, there was a fine massive gravity in his face, which I did not venture to disturb.

"You see, sir, when she was a child, she used to talk to me a deal about the sea, and about them coasts where the sea got to be dark blue, and to lay a shining and a shining in the sun. When she was – lost, I know'd in my mind, as he would take her to them countries. I know'd in my mind, as he'd have told her wonders of 'em, and how she was to be a lady theer, and how he first got her to listen to him along o' sech like. I went across-channel to France, and landed theer, as if I'd fell down from the skies. I found out a English gentleman, as was in authority, and told him I was going to seek my niece. He got me them papers as I wanted fur to carry me through – I doen't rightly know how they're called – and he would have give me money, but that I was thankful to have no need on. I thank him kind, for all he done, I'm sure! I told him, best as I was able, what my gratitoode was, and went away through France, fur to seek my niece."

"Alone, and on foot?"

"Mostly a-foot; sometimes in carts along with people going to market; sometimes in empty coaches. Many mile a day a-foot, and often with some poor soldier or another, travelling fur to see his friends. I couldn't talk to him, nor he to me; but we was company for one another, too, along the dusty roads. When I come to any town, I found the inn, and waited about the yard till some one came by (some one mostly did) as know'd English. Then I told how that I was on my way to seek my niece, and they told me what manner of gentlefolks was in the house, and I waited to see any as seemed like her, going in or out. When it warn't Em'ly, I went on agen. By little and little, when I come to a new village or that, among the poor people, I found they know'd about me.

They would set me down at their cottage doors, and give me what-not fur to eat and drink, and show me where to sleep. And many a woman, Mas'r Davy, as has had a daughter of about Em'ly's age, I've found a-waiting for me, at Our Saviour's Cross outside the village, fur to do me sim'lar kindnesses. Some has had daughters as was dead. And God only knows how good them mothers was to me!"

I laid my trembling hand upon the hand he put before his face. "Thankee, sir, doen't take no notice.

"At last I come to the sea. It warn't hard, you may suppose, for a seafaring man like me to work his way over to Italy. When I got theer, I wandered on as I had done afore. I got news of her being seen among them Swiss mountains yonder. I made for them mountains, day and night. Ever so fur as I went, ever so fur them mountains seemed to shift away from me. But I come up with 'em, and I crossed 'em. I never doubted her. No! Not a bit! On'y let her see my face – on'y let her heer my voice – on'y let my stanning still afore her bring to her thoughts the home she had fled away from, and the child she had been – and if she had growed to be a royal lady, she'd have fell down at my feet! I know'd it well! I bought a country dress to put upon her. To put that dress upon her, and to cast off what she wore – to take her on my arm again, and wander towards home – to stop sometimes upon the road, and heal her bruised feet and her worse-bruised heart – was all I thowt of now. But, Mas'r Davy, it warn't to be – not yet! I was too late, and they was gone. Wheer, I couldn't learn. Some said heer, some said theer. I travelled heer, and I travelled theer, but I found no Em'ly, and I travelled home."

"How long ago?"

"A matter o' fower days. I sighted the old boat arter dark, and I never could have thowt, I'm sure, that the old boat would have been so strange!"

From some pocket in his breast, he took out with a very careful hand, a small paper bundle containing two or three letters or little packets, which he laid upon the table.

"The faithful creetur Mrs. Gummidge gave me these. This first one come afore I had been gone a week. A fifty pound Bank note, in a sheet of paper, directed to me, and put underneath

the door in the night. She tried to hide her writing, but she couldn't hide it from me! This one come to Missis Gummidge, two or three months ago. Five pounds."

It was untouched like the previous sum, and he refolded both.

"Is that another letter in your hand?"

"It's money too, sir. Ten pound, you see. And wrote inside, 'From a true friend.' But the two first was put underneath the door, and this come by the post, day afore yesterday. I'm going to seek her at the postmark."

He showed it to me. It was a town on the Upper Rhine. He had found out, at Yarmouth, some foreign dealers who knew that country, and they had drawn him a rude map on paper, which he could very well understand.

I asked him how Ham was?

"He works as bold as a man can. He's never been heerd fur to complain. But my belief is ('twixt ourselves) as it has cut him deep. Well! Having seen you to-night, Mas'r Davy (and that doos me good!), I shall away betimes to-morrow morning. You have seen what I've got heer;" putting his hand on where the little packet lay; "all that troubles me is, to think that any harm might come to me, afore this money was give back. If I was to die, and it was lost, or stole, or elseways made away with, and it was never know'd by him but what I'd accepted of it, I believe the t'other wureld wouldn't hold me! I believe I must come back!"

He rose, and I rose too. We grasped each other by the hand again, and as we went out into the rigorous night, everything seemed to be hushed in reverence for him, when he resumed his solitary journey through the snow.

CHAPTER V

All this time I had gone on loving Dora harder than ever. If I may so express it, I was steeped in Dora. I was not merely over head and ears in love with her; I was saturated through and through. I took night walks to Norwood where she lived, and perambulated round and round the house and garden for hours together; looking through crevices in the palings, using violent exertions to get my chain above the rusty nails on the top, blowing kisses at the lights in the windows, and romantically calling on the night to shield my Dora. – I don't exactly know from what – I suppose from fire – perhaps from mice, to which she had a great objection.

Dora had a discreet friend, comparatively stricken in years – almost of the ripe age of twenty, I should say – whose name was Miss Mills. Dora called her Julia, and she was the bosom friend of Dora. Happy Miss Mills!

One day Miss Mills said, "Dora is coming to stay with me. She is coming the day after to-morrow. If you would like to call, I am sure papa would be happy to see you."

I passed three days in a luxury of wretchedness, and at last, arrayed for the purpose at a vast expense, I went to Miss Mills's fraught with a declaration.

Mr. Mills was not at home. I didn't expect he would be. Nobody wanted *him.* Miss Mills was at home. Miss Mills would do.

I was shown into a room up-stairs, where Miss Mills and Dora were. Dora's little dog Jip was there. Miss Mills was copying music, and Dora was painting flowers. – What were my feelings when I recognized flowers I had given her!

Miss Mills was very glad to see me, and very sorry her papa was not at home: though I thought we all bore that with fortitude. Miss Mills was conversational for a few minutes, and then, laying down her pen, got up and left the room.

I began to think I would put it off till to-morrow.

"I hope your poor horse was not tired, when he got home at night from that pic-nic," said Dora, lifting up her beautiful eyes. "It was a long way for him."

I began to think I would do it to-day.

"It was a long way for *him,* for *he* had nothing to uphold him on the journey."

"Wasn't he fed, poor thing?" asked Dora.

I began to think I would put it off till to-morrow.

"Ye-yes, he was well taken care of. I mean he had not the unutterable happiness that I had in being so near you."

I saw now that I was in for it, and it must be done on the spot.

"I don't know why you should care for being near me," said Dora, "or why you should call it a happiness. But of course you don't mean what you say. Jip, you naughty boy, come here!"

I don't know how I did it, but I did it in a moment. I intercepted Jip. I had Dora in my arms. I was full of eloquence. I never stopped for a word. I told her how I loved her. I told her I should die without her. I told her that I idolized and worshipped her. – Jip barked madly all the time. My eloquence increased and I said, if she would like me to die for her, she had but to say the word, and I was ready. I had loved her to distraction every minute, day and night, since I first set eyes upon her. I loved her at that minute to distraction. I should always love her, every minute, to distraction. Lovers had loved before, and lovers would love again; but no lover had ever loved, might, could, would, or should, ever love, as I loved Dora. – The more I raved, the more Jip barked. Each of us, in his own way, got more mad every moment. Well, well! Dora and I were sitting on the sofa by-and-by, quiet enough, and Jip was lying in her lap, winking peacefully at me. It was off my mind. I was in a state of perfect rapture. Dora and I were engaged.

Being poor, I felt it necessary the next time I went to my darling, to expatiate on that unfortunate drawback. I soon carried desolation into the bosom of our joys – not that I meant to do it, but that I was so full of the subject – by asking Dora, without the smallest preparation, if she could love a beggar?

"How can you ask me anything so foolish? Love a beggar!"

"Dora, my own dearest, *I* am a beggar!"

"How can you be such a silly thing," replied Dora, slapping my hand, "as to sit there, telling such stories? I'll make Jip bite you if you are so ridiculous."

But I looked so serious, that Dora began to cry. She did nothing but exclaim Oh dear! Oh dear! And oh, she was so frightened! And where was Julia Mills! And oh, take her to Julia Mills, and go away, please! until I was almost beside myself.

43

I thought I had killed her. I sprinkled water on her face. I went down on my knees. I plucked at my hair. I implored her forgiveness. I besought her to look up. I ravaged Miss Mills's work-box for a smelling-bottle, and in my agony of mind applied an ivory needle-case instead, and dropped all the needles over Dora.

At last, I got Dora to look at me, with a horrified expression, which I gradually soothed until it was only loving, and her soft, pretty cheek was lying against mine.

"Is your heart mine still, dear Dora?"

"Oh, yes! Oh, yes, it's all yours. Oh, don't be dreadful!"

I dreadful! To Dora!

"Don't talk about being poor, and working hard! Oh, don't, don't!"

"My dearest love, the crust well earned –"

"Oh, yes; but I don't want to hear any more about crusts. And after we are married, Jip must have a mutton-chop every day at twelve, or he'll die!"

I was charmed with her childish, winning way, and I fondly explained to her that Jip should have his mutton-chop with his accustomed regularity.

When we had been engaged some half a year or so, Dora delighted me by asking me to give

her that cookery-book I had once spoken of, and to show her how to keep housekeeping accounts, as I had once promised I would. I brought the volume with me on my next visit (I got it prettily bound, first, to make it look less dry and more inviting); and showed her an old housekeeping-book of my aunt's, and gave her a set of tablets, and a pretty little pencil-case, and a box of leads, to practise house-keeping with.

But the cookery-book made Dora's head ache, and the figures made her cry. They wouldn't add up, she said. So she rubbed them out, and drew little nosegays, and likenesses of me and Jip, all over the tablets.

Time went on, and at last, here in this hand of mine I held the wedding licence. There were the two names in the sweet old visionary connexion, David Copperfield and Dora Spenlow; and there in the corner was that parental Institution the Stamp-office, looking down upon our union; and there, in the printed form of words, was the Archbishop of Canterbury invoking a blessing on us, and doing it as cheap as could possibly be expected!

I doubt whether two young birds could have known less about keeping house, than I and my pretty Dora did. We had a servant, of course. She kept house for us. We had an awful time of it with Mary Anne.

Her name was Paragon. Her nature was represented to us, when we engaged her, as being feebly expressed in her name. She had a written character, as large as a Proclamation; and, according to this document, could do everything of a domestic nature that I ever heard of, and a great many things that I never did hear of. She was a woman in the prime of life: of a severe countenance; and subject (particularly in the arms) to a sort of perpetual measles. She had a cousin in the Life Guards, with such long legs that he looked like the afternoon shadow of somebody else. She was warranted sober and honest. And I am therefore willing to believe that she was in a fit when we found her under the boiler; and that the deficient teaspoons were attributable to the dustman. She was the cause of our first little quarrel.

"My dearest life," I said one day to Dora, "do you think Mary Anne has any idea of time?"

"Why, Doady?"

"My love, because it's five, and we were to have dined at four."

My little wife came and sat upon my knee, to coax me to be quiet, and drew a line with her pencil down the middle of my nose: but I couldn't dine off that, though it was very agreeable.

"Don't you think, my dear, it would be better for you to remonstrate with Mary Anne?"

"Oh no, please! I couldn't, Doady!"

"Why not, my love?"

"Oh, because I am such a little goose, and she knows I am!"

45

I thought this sentiment so incompatible with the establishment of any system of check on Mary Anne, that I frowned a little.

"My precious wife, we must be serious sometimes. Come! Sit down on this chair, close beside me! Give me the pencil! There! Now let us talk sensibly. You know, dear;" what a little hand it was to hold, and what a tiny wedding-ring it was to see! "You know, my love, it is not exactly comfortable to have to go out without one's dinner. Now, is it?"

"N – n – no!" replied Dora, faintly.

"My love, how you tremble!"

"Because I KNOW you're going to scold me."

"My sweet, I am only going to reason."

"Oh, but reasoning is worse than scolding! I didn't marry to be reasoned with. If you meant to reason with such a poor little thing as I am, you ought to have told me so, you cruel boy!"

"Now, my own Dora, you are childish, and are talking nonsense. You must remember, I am sure, that I was obliged to go out yesterday when dinner was half over; and that, the day before, I was made quite unwell by being obliged to eat underdone veal in a hurry; to-day, I don't dine at all – and I am afraid to say how long we waited for breakfast – and *then* the water didn't boil. I don't mean to reproach you, my dear, but this is not comfortable."

"I wonder, I do, at your making such ungrateful speeches. When you know that the other day, when you said you would like a little bit of fish, I went out myself, miles and miles, and ordered it, to surprise you."

"And it was very kind of you, my own darling, and I felt it so much that I wouldn't on any account have mentioned that you bought a salmon – which was too much for two. Or that it cost one pound six – which was more than we can afford."

"You enjoyed it very much," sobbed Dora. "And you said I was a mouse."

"And I'll say so again, my love, a thousand times!"

I said it a thousand times, and more, and went on saying it until Mary Anne's cousin deserted into our coal-hole, and was brought out, to our great amazement, by a piquet of his companions in arms, who took him away handcuffed, in a procession that covered our front-garden with disgrace.

Everybody we had anything to do with, seemed to cheat us. Our appearance in a shop was a signal for the damaged goods to be brought out immediately. If we bought a lobster, it was full of water. All our meat turned out tough, and there was hardly any crust to our loaves. As to the washerwoman pawning the clothes, and coming in a state of penitent intoxication to apologize, I suppose that might have happened several times to anybody. Also the chimney

47

on fire, the parish engine, and perjury on the part of the Beadle. But I apprehend we were personally unfortunate in our page: whose principal function was to quarrel with the cook and who lived in a hail of saucepan-lids. We wanted to get rid of him, but he was very much attached to us, and wouldn't go, until one day he stole Dora's watch, and spent the produce (he was always a weak-minded boy) in riding up and down between London and Uxbridge outside the coach. He was taken to the Police Office, on the completion of his fifteenth journey; when four-and-sixpence, and a second-hand fife which he couldn't play, were found upon his person.

He was tried and ordered to be transported. Even then he couldn't be quiet, but was always writing us letters; and he wanted so much to see Dora before he went away, that Dora went to visit him, and fainted when she found herself inside the iron bars. I had no peace of my life until he was expatriated, and made (as I afterwards heard) a shepherd of, "up the country" somewhere; I have no geographical idea where.

"I am very sorry for all this, Doady," said Dora. "Will you call me a name I want you to call me?"

"What is it, my dear?"

"It's a stupid name – Child-wife. When you are going to be angry with me, say to yourself 'it's only my Child-wife.' When I am very disappointing, say, 'I knew, a long time ago, that she would make but a Child-wife.' When you miss what you would like me to be, and what I should like to be, and what I think I never can be, say, 'Still my foolish Child-wife loves me.' For indeed I do."

I invoke the innocent figure that I dearly loved, to come out of the mists and shadows of the Past, and to turn its gentle head towards me once again, and to bear witness that it was made happy by what I answered.

CHAPTER VI

I heard a footstep on the stairs one day. I knew it to be Mr. Peggotty's. It came nearer, nearer, rushed into the room.

"Mas'r Davy, I've found her! I thank my Heavenly Father for having guided of me in His own ways to my darling!"

"You have made up your mind as to the future, good friend?"

"Yes, Mas'r Davy, theer's mighty countries, fur from heer. Our future life lays over the sea."

As he gave me both his hands, hurrying to return to the one charge of his noble existence, I thought of Ham and who would break the intelligence to him? Mr. Peggotty thought of everything. He had already written to the poor fellow, and had the letter in the pocket of his rough coat, ready for the post. I asked him for it, and said I would go down to Yarmouth, and talk to Ham myself before I gave it him, and prepare him for its contents. He thanked me very earnestly, and we parted, with the understanding that I would go down by the Mail that same night. In the evening I started.

"Don't you think that," I asked the coachman, in the first stage out of London, "a very remark-able sky? I don't remember to have ever seen one like it."

"Nor I. That's wind, sir. There'll be mischief done at sea before long."

It was a murky confusion of flying clouds tossed up into most remarkable heaps, through which the wild moon seemed to plunge headlong, as if, in a dread disturbance of the laws of nature, she had lost her way. There had been a wind all day; and it was rising then, with an extraordinary great sound. In another hour it had much increased, and the sky was more overcast, and it blew hard.

But, as the night advanced, it came on to blow, harder and harder. I had been in Yarmouth when the seamen said it blew great guns, but I had never known the like of this, or anything approaching to it.

The tremendous sea itself, when I came to my journey's end, confounded me. As the high watery walls came rolling in, and tumbled into surf, I seemed to see a rending and upheaving of all nature.

Not finding Ham among the people whom this memorable wind had brought together on the beach, I made my way to his house. I learned that he had gone, on a job of shipwright's work, some miles away, but that he would be back to-morrow morning, in good time.

So, I went back to the inn; and when I had washed and dressed, and tried to sleep, but in vain, it was late in the afternoon. I had not sat five minutes by the coffee-room fire, when the waiter coming to stir it, told me that two colliers had gone down, with all hands, a few miles off; and that some other ships had been seen labouring hard in the Roads, and trying, in great distress, to keep off shore. Mercy on them, and on all poor sailors, said he, if we had another night like the last!

I could not eat, I could not sit still, I could not continue stedfast to anything. My dinner went away almost untasted, and I tried to refresh myself with a glass or two of wine. In vain. I walked to and fro, tried to read an old gazetteer, listened to the awful noises: looked at faces, scenes, and figures in the fire. At length the ticking of the undisturbed clock on the wall, tormented me to that degree that I resolved to go to bed.

For hours, I lay in bed listening to the wind and water; imagining, now, that I heard shrieks out at sea; now, that I distinctly heard the firing of signal guns; now, the fall of houses in the town. At length, my restlessness attained to such a pitch, that I hurried on my clothes, and went down-stairs.

In the large kitchen, all the inn servants and some other watchers were clustered together. One man asked me when I went in among them whether I thought the souls of the collier-crews who had gone down, were out in the storm?

There was a dark gloom in my lonely chamber, when I at length returned to it; but I was tired now, and, getting into bed again, fell into the depths of sleep until broad day; when I was aroused, at eight or nine o'clock, by some one knocking and calling at my door.

"What is the matter?"

"A wreck! Close by!"

"What wreck?"

"A schooner, from Spain or Portugal, laden with fruit and wine. Make haste, sir, if you want to see her! It's thought, down on the beach, she'll go to pieces every moment."

I wrapped myself in my clothes as quickly as I could, and ran into the street, where numbers of people were before me, all running in one direction – to the beach.

When I got there, – in the difficulty of hearing anything but wind and waves, and in the crowd, and the unspeakable confusion, and my first breathless efforts to stand against the weather, I was so confused that I looked out to sea for the wreck, and saw nothing but the foaming heads of the great waves. A boatman laid a hand upon my arm, and pointed. Then, I saw it, close in upon us!

One mast was broken short off, six or eight feet from the deck, and lay over the side, entangled in a maze of sail and rigging; and all that ruin, as the ship rolled and beat – which she did with a violence quite inconceivable – beat the side as if it would stave it in. Some efforts were being made, to cut this portion of the wreck away; for, as the ship, which was broadside on, turned towards us in her rolling, I plainly descried her people at work with axes – especially one active figure with long curling hair. But, a great cry, audible even above the wind and water, rose from the shore; the sea, sweeping over the wreck, made a clean breach, and carried men, spars, casks, planks, bulwarks, heaps of such toys, into the boiling surge.

The second mast was yet standing, with the rags of a sail, and a wild confusion of broken cordage flapping to and fro. The ship had struck once, the same boatman said, and then lifted in and struck again. I understood him to add that she was parting amidships. As he spoke, there was another great cry of pity from the beach. Four men arose with the wreck out of the deep, clinging to the rigging of the remaining mast; uppermost, the active figure with the curling hair.

There was a bell on board; and as the ship rolled and dashed, this bell rang; and its sound, the knell of those unhappy men, was borne towards us on the wind. Again we lost her, and again she rose. Two of the four men were gone.

I noticed that some new sensation moved the people on the beach, and I saw them part, and Ham come breaking through them to the front.

Instantly, I ran to him, for I divined that he meant to wade off with a rope. I held him back with both arms; and implored the men not to listen to him, not to let him stir from that sand! Another cry arose; and we saw the cruel sail, with blow on blow, beat off the lower of the two men, and fly up in triumph round the active figure left alone upon the mast.

Against such a sight, and against such determination as that of the calmly desperate man who was already accustomed to lead half the people present, I might as hopefully have entreated the wind.

I was swept away to some distance, where the people around me made me stay; urging, as I confusedly perceived, that he was bent on going, with help or without, and that I should endanger the precautions for his safety by troubling those with whom they rested. I saw hurry on the beach, and men running with ropes, and penetrating into a circle of figures that hid him from me. Then, I saw him standing alone, in a seaman's frock and trowsers: a rope in his hand: another round his body: and several of the best men holding to the latter.

The wreck was breaking up. I saw that she was parting in the middle, and that the life of the solitary man upon the mast hung by a thread. He had a singular red cap on, not like a sailor's cap, but of a finer colour; and as the few planks between him and destruction rolled and bulged, and as his death-knell rung, he was seen by all of us to wave this cap. I saw him do it now, and thought I was going distracted, when his action brought an old remembrance to my mind of a once dear friend – *the* once dear friend – Steerforth.

Ham watched the sea, until there was a great retiring wave; when he dashed in after it, and in a moment was buffeting with the water, rising with the hills, falling with the valleys, lost beneath the foam: borne in towards the shore, borne on towards the ship. At length he neared the wreck. He was so near, that with one more of his vigorous strokes he would be clinging to it, – when, a high green vast hill-side of water, moving on shoreward, from beyond the ship, he seemed to leap up into it with a mightly bound – and the ship was gone!

They drew him to my very feet – insensible – dead. He was carried to the nearest house; and every means of restoration were tried; but he had been beaten to death by the great wave, and his generous heart was stilled for ever.

As I sat beside the bed, when hope was abandoned and all was done, a fisherman, who had known me when Emily and I were children, and ever since, whispered my name at the door. "Sir, will you come over yonder?"

The old remembrance that had been recalled to me, was in his look, and I asked him:

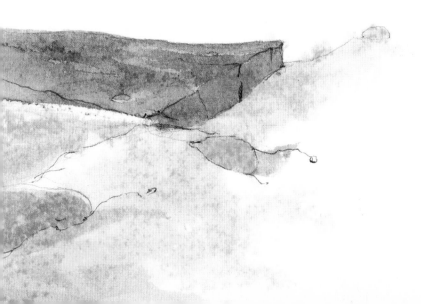

"Has a body come ashore?"

"Yes."

"Do I know it?"

He answered nothing. But, he led me to the shore. And on that part of it where she and I had looked for shells, two children – on that part of it where some lighter fragments of the old boat, blown down last night, had been scattered by the wind – among the ruins of the home he had wronged – I saw him lying with his head upon his arm, as I had often seen him lie at school.

AFTERWORD

During the last sixteen years of his life the novelist Charles Dickens, who lived from 1812 to 1870, gave many public readings from his own works. By then he was a very famous author. His early books, such as *The Pickwick Papers*, had been bestsellers on their first appearance and were still as popular as ever. Every new novel he wrote was eagerly awaited, and so were the shorter "Christmas Stories" he produced almost every year. These stories included the well-known *A Christmas Carol*, which Dickens used for his first public reading to an audience.

It was so successful that he went on to adapt several of his other works for performance all over the British Isles, and in a 1867-68 tour of the United States. This book contains the text Dickens prepared for his reading from the novel *David Copperfield*, first published in monthly installments in the years 1849-50. It was a particular favourite of his own, perhaps because the story is partly based on his own childhood and youth. The reading he took from it was one of his favourites too, and proved extremely popular with audiences. Dickens delivered it with great dramatic feeling. The daughter of the novelist William Makepeace Thackeray wrote that when Dickens came to the scene of the storm and the shipwreck, "finally we were all breathless watching from the shore, and a great wave seemed to fall splashing on the platform from overhead." These "readings" were really more like dramatic entertainments. Friends of Dickens, among them the famous actor William Macready, often said that if he had not been a novelist he could have had a stage career.

Even as a small child Charles Dickens was fascinated by theatrical performances, and he owned a little toy theatre with cut-out figures for the characters. In those days people made their own entertainment at home, and the Dickens family would amuse themselves in the evenings by performing songs, recitations, and scenes from plays. Young Charles was good at singing comic songs, accompanied on the piano by his sister Fanny. He carried on the same tradition when he was grown up with a family of his own, and the Dickens children (seven boys and two girls) acted plays directed by their father on Christmas and Twelfth Night. Dickens was also a leading figure in an amateur dramatics company which he formed with some of his literary friends in London. They put on plays to raise money for charity. Dickens directed many productions, taking prominent parts himself, and the company even performed twice in front of Queen Victoria. His own first public readings were for charity too, and raised a great deal of money for causes like the Hospital for Sick Children in London. Later on, when he needed money for himself to support his large family as they were growing up, he charged for entrance to the readings and made almost a second career out of them, touring the country for up to three months at a time.

Charles Dickens put much thought into preparing his readings. There had already been dramatized versions of his novels on the London stage; he did not make these stage adaptations himself, but for his public readings he personally abridged his texts with great care, choosing scenes that would make self-contained stories, adapting, rewriting, adding underlinings to certain words and phrases for emphasis. *David Copperfield* in full is a long novel, with several strands of plot. For the reading, Dickens chose to concentrate on the sad story of the narrator David's childhood sweetheart Little Em'ly, who runs away with his old school friend Steerforth. He also brought in some of the comedy of the Micawber family and the tale of David's love for pretty, silly Dora, but Emily's story was to be the main part. Dickens wrote himself a note when planning the reading: "First chapter funny. Then on *to Emily*."

Everything about the readings was precisely timed. They generally lasted about two hours: First there was a fairly long reading from one novel, then an interval, and then a shorter reading, usually a comic one. Dickens added stage directions to himself in the text. In *David Copperfield*, for instance, he wrote comments in the margin such as "Solemnly, slowly, measuredly, and with feeling," "Looking up occasionally with a sneer," "Facial expression. Elevating eyebrows." The "facial expression" was important to him. He used to rehearse the readings for hours on end, practising different voices aloud, watching his gestures and the faces he made in a mirror. All this was a vital part of the entertainment, and he would never allow people to sit behind him where they could not see his face during the performance. For these were genuine stage performances and not just readings. Dickens had a great gift for mimicry and altered his voice for each character, making his audiences feel they actually saw the various people in the story before their eyes.

When he was on tour with the readings, Dickens would usually travel by rail, taking his own "stage props" to be put up in the large public halls where he performed. He had a maroon screen behind him, a maroon carpet on the platform, and gas lighting to cast a strong, dramatic light on his face. On one occasion the gas lighting was not properly adjusted, and looked likely to burn through the copper wires that were part of it. Dickens saw what was happening, worked out how long the wires would last, and shortened his text as he went along so that he would finish just before they were about to give way. The audience never noticed anything wrong.

Dickens also took his own desk on tour. It was a prop for him to lean on, rather than a place to rest his text, because he knew the words of his readings by heart. Sometimes he merely opened the text he had brought, closed it again, and delivered his whole performance from memory. Most of the members of the audience who flocked to hear him knew the books almost as well as he did, and if he added something, perhaps a new joke that was not in the original, they noticed and enjoyed the change.

He told his audiences they must feel free to laugh or cry as if they were by their own firesides, and we know that they did just that. During a particularly sad scene, one man shed tears and then "covered his face with both hands, and laid it down on the back of the seat before him, and really shook with emotion." There was enthusiastic applause at the end of every show — for, in a phrase Dickens once used, this was "real show business." He cared a great deal about the audience's reaction, and once declined to read *A Christmas Carol* to the queen herself, fearing that he would not get his usual good effect if there were only a very few people listening.

Dickens was already middle-aged when he began to give his readings, and he put so much energy into them that they often left him feeling exhausted. It was a tiring business going from city to city in Great Britain, Ireland, and the United States, sometimes giving a series of eighty or more evening performances with very few free days in between, and he was still editing a popular magazine and writing new novels as well. Rail travel itself tired him, especially after he was in a terrible railway accident. He was uninjured himself, and worked to help the other victims of the disaster, but felt severely shaken afterwards. His last series of readings, a short "farewell tour" early in 1870, was given against medical advice, and one of his sons believed the strain helped to bring on his death in June of that year, before he was yet sixty.

However, he loved giving the readings and meeting his enthusiastic audiences, and would go on stage even when feeling unwell rather than disappoint them. He was pleased when one woman approached him after a reading and asked, "Mr. Dickens, will you let me touch the hand that has filled my house with many friends?" Hers would have been a typical reaction, for readers felt that the characters Charles Dickens created were as real as living people. It must have been a wonderful experience to hear the author himself give fresh life to those characters.

Anthea Bell

Illustrations and Afterword copyright © 1995 by Michael Neugebauer Verlag AG, Gossau Zürich, Switzerland.

The text of this edition has been used with the kind permission of Oxford University Press and has been taken from the book *Sikes and Nancy and Other Public Readings* by Charles Dickens, edited and with an introduction and notes by Philip Collins.

First published in the United States, Canada, Great Britain, Australia, and New Zealand in 1995 by North-South Books, an imprint of Nord-Süd Verlag AG, Gossau Zürich, Switzerland.

Distributed in the United States by North-South Books Inc., New York.

Library of Congress Cataloging-in-Publication Data is available.
A CIP catalogue record for this book is available from The British Library.
ISBN 1-55858-453-6 (trade binding) 10 9 8 7 6 5 4 3 2 1
ISBN 1-55858-454-4 (library binding) 10 9 8 7 6 5 4 3 2 1
Printed in Italy